DENNIS NOLAN

Sea of Dreams

A NEAL PORTER BOOK
ROARING BROOK PRESS
NEW YORK

For Evie

Copyright © 2011 by Dennis Nolan
A Neal Porter Book
Published by Roaring Brook Press
Roaring Brook Press is a division of Holtzbrinck Publishing Holdings Limited Partnership
175 Fifth Avenue, New York, New York 10010
mackids.com

Library of Congress Cataloging-in-Publication Data

Nolan, Dennis, 1945–
  Sea of dreams / Dennis Nolan.
    p. cm.
  "A Neal Porter book."
  Summary: A wordless picture book featuring a sandcastle that takes on a
life of its own.
  ISBN 978-1-59643-470-7
  [1. Sandcastles—Fiction. 2. Stories without words.] I. Title.

PZ7.N678Se 2011
[E]—dc22
                                                            2010037815

Roaring Brook Press books are available for special promotions and premiums.
For details contact: Director of Special Markets, Holtzbrinck Publishers.

First edition 2011
Printed in the United States of America by Phoenix Color Corp. d/b/a Lehigh Phoenix, Rockaway, New Jerey

3 5 7 9 8 6 4 2

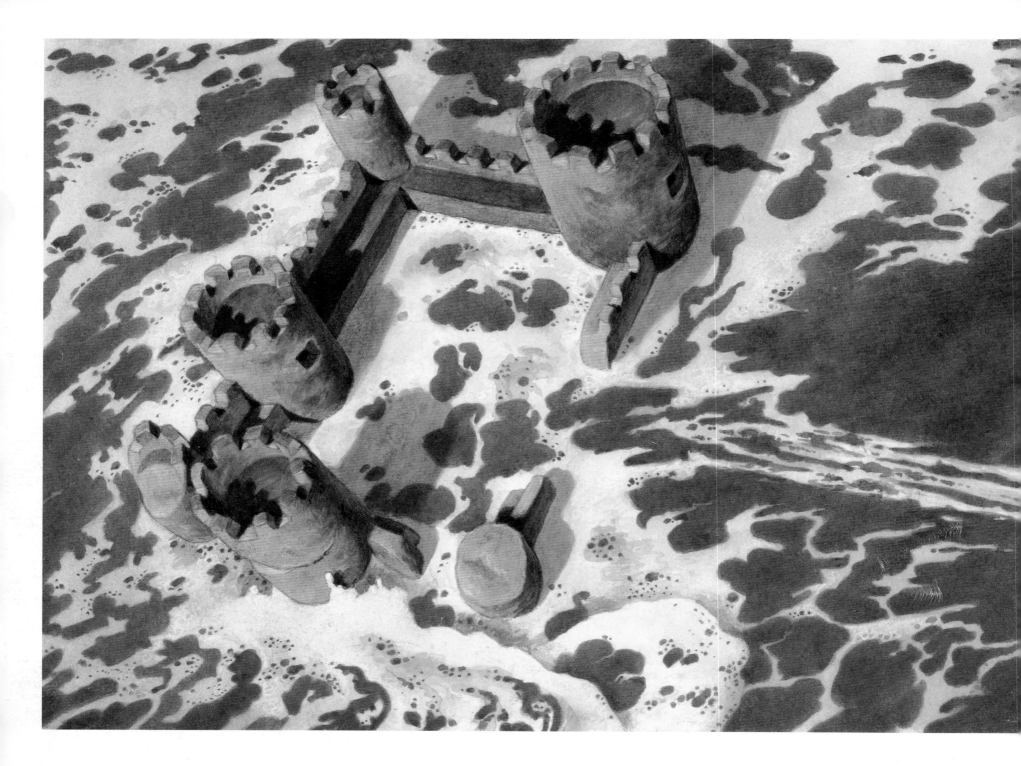